JESSICA'S MOTHER

JESSICA'S MOTHER

BY

HESBA STRETTON

THE AUTHOR OF "JESSICA'S FIRST PRAYER", "ALONE IN
LONDON", AND "LITTLE MEG'S CHILDREN."

CURIOSMITH

MINNEAPOLIS

Published by Curiosmith.
P. O. Box 390293, Minneapolis, Minnesota, 55439.
Internet: curiosmith.com.
E-mail: shopkeeper@curiosmith.com.

Previously published by Sunday at Home in 1867.

Scripture verses are from *The Holy Bible*, King James Version.

Definitions are from *Webster's Revised Unabridged Dictionary*, 1828 and 1913.

ISBN 9781935626763

CONTENTS

CHAPTER I

GREAT PLANS

It was a gloomy Sunday in the gloomiest part of the year, when the fog hung over London day and night, only lifting itself off a little for two or three hours about noon time. The bells which rang from the church towers might have been chiming from some region above the clouds, so distant they sounded and so hidden were the belfries in which they hung.

In the early part of the day the congregations went to and from their various places of worship, with a feeling of somber depression at the long continuance of the gloom; but after nightfall the darkness was only natural, and though the lamps gave but little light, and shone merely like yellow balls in the fog, the passengers in the street moved more briskly and talked more cheerfully than in the morning. Here and there the brilliantly illuminated windows of some church or chapel cast a pleasant gleam upon the pavement, and the open doors seemed to invite any cold or weary passer-by to enter into its light and warmth; but as if these buildings, the temples of God, were designed only for the rich, and for those who had comfort enough in their own dwellings, it was noticeable that but a very scanty sprinkling of worshippers dressed in vile raiment were to be seen among the congregations, though there was no lack of those who wore goodly apparel and gay clothing.

The fashionable chapel of which Daniel Standring was the chapel-keeper was no exception to the general rule, for there were no poor to be found in it. There was within it every appliance of comfort and style such as could give satisfaction to a wealthy congregation. The oak pews were high enough for the head of an occasional slumberer to repose in quiet indulgence, and they were well lined and carpeted and cushioned. The shades for the lamps toned down their light to a clear, yet soft, lustre; and the apparatus for heating the building was of the most efficient kind.

The crowds who flocked to hear the minister were increasing every Sunday, and Daniel Standring had, with some reluctance, yielded to the necessity of sharing his office of pew-opener with a colleague; a man, however, of less dignity and solemnity of deportment than himself, and who was quite willing to look up to him as a superior. Moreover, the old members of the church, the "carriage people" especially, recognized him only as their chapel-keeper, and entrusted any message or any commission to him alone; and he also retained the charge of attending upon the vestry. The other man was no more than a subordinate; and after awhile he was reconciled to his division of office.

There had been two things much talked about among the people for some time past: the first, that the minister himself should have a colleague found for him; and the second, that a larger and still more fashionable chapel should be built.

As to the colleague there were several difficulties in

the way, the chief one being to find such a preacher as would attract the same congregation as those which came in crowds to listen to the minister; for it was found that whenever it was known that he would be absent from his pulpit the numbers dwindled away, until during his yearly holiday the chapel would seem almost empty, compared to the throng of curious and eager listeners, who hung upon his words, and scarcely dared to sigh over his representations of their misery and peril, lest they should miss hearing a single syllable of the eloquence which described it.

Still every member of the congregation said it was essential that a colleague should be found for their beloved pastor before he had quite worn himself out; and great blame was thrown back upon the small provincial church which five-and-twenty years ago had thrust him, a mere youth of twenty, upon the exhausting duties of the ministry. As for the second subject, it was settled without much difficulty, for only money, not a man, was wanted; and upon the vestry table there was a subscription-list, already promising some thousands of pounds, and beside it lay the plans for the new chapel, drawn up by an eminent architect.

The chapel doors had been opened by Daniel, and the gas toned down to precisely the brilliance and softness which the congregation loved, especially the lamps on each side of the pulpit, which shed a revealing light upon the minister's thoughtful face, and upon his dark hair just tinged with gray. In the vestry Jessica had just given a final and delicate stroke of dusting, and was wiping the

large pulpit Bible and hymn-book with her clean pocket-
handkerchief, ready for Daniel to carry up into the pulpit while the organist was playing the opening voluntary,
which he did with so solemn and ministerial an aspect,
that a stranger, not accustomed to the etiquette of the
place, might be betrayed into the supposition that he was
the minister himself.

Daniel was waiting now in the porch like some faithful steward, ready to receive his master's guests; and as
carriage after carriage rolled up, almost a smile of satisfaction softened his rigid features. The minister's children had passed him with a smile and a nod, and he had
shut the door of their pew in the corner, so he knew that
the minister was come, and putting a little additional
briskness into his manner, he looked out for seats for the
strangers who were filling the aisles, at the same time
listening for the first notes of the organ.

The minister had entered the vestry just as Jessica
had finished wiping the imaginary dust off the Bible and
hymn book, and he drew his chair up close to the fire, as
if coming through the fog had chilled him. He looked sad
and downcast, and his head sank forward upon his breast.
For a minute Jessica stood behind his chair in silence,
and then she stretched out her hand, a small thin hand
still, and laid it timidly upon his arm.

"Jessica," said the minister, covering her small palm
with his scholarly hand, "I am sorrowful tonight, and I
have great heaviness of heart. Tell me, my child, do you
understand what I preach about in my pulpit?"

"Oh, no, no!" answered Jessica, shaking her head

deprecatingly, "only when you say God, and Jesus Christ, and heaven! I know what you mean by them."

"Do you?" said the minister, with a very tender smile; "and do I say them often, Jessica?"

"Sometimes they come over and over again," replied Jessica, "and then I feel very glad, because I know what you are preaching about. There is always God in your sermons, but sometimes there isn't Jesus Christ and heaven."

"And what do I mean by God, and Jesus Christ, and heaven?" he asked.

"I don't know anything but what you've taught me," said Jessica, folding her brown hands meekly over one another; "you've told me that God is the Father of our souls, and Jesus Christ is our elder brother, who came down from heaven to save us, and heaven is the home of God, where we shall all go if we love and serve him. I don't know any more than that."

"It is enough!" said the minister, lifting up his head with a brighter look; "one soul has learned the truth from me. God bless you, Jessica, and keep you in his fear and love for evermore."

As he spoke, the deep tones of the organ fell upon their ears, and the vestry door was opened by Daniel, coming for the pulpit books. There was an air of solemn pride upon his face, and he bowed lower than usual to his minister.

"There's a vast crush of people tonight, sir," he said; "the aisles and the galleries are all full, and there's a many standing at the door yet who will have to go away, for there's no room for them."

The minister covered his face with his hands and

DANIEL AND JESSICA IN THE VESTRY BEFORE SERVICE.

shivered, with the cold no doubt; and Daniel and Jessica were leaving the vestry when they were called back by his voice speaking in husky and agitated tones.

"Standring," he said, "I have something of importance to say to you after the service this evening, so come back here as soon as the congregation is gone. And, Jessica, take care to sit in your own place, where I can see you; for I will preach about Jesus Christ and heaven tonight."

Jessica answered only by a little nod, and left the

vestry by a door which did not open into the chapel. In a minute or two afterwards she was making her way up the crowded aisles to her usual seat at the foot of the pulpit steps, where, with her head thrown back, her face lifted itself up to the minister's gaze.

She had just time to settle herself and glance at the minister's children, who were looking out for her, when the last quiet notes of the organ ceased, and the vestry door opened. The minister mounted the stairs slowly, and with his head bent down; but as soon as he was in the pulpit he looked round upon the faces whose eyes were all fastened upon him.

Many of the faces he knew, and had seen thus upraised to him for scores of Sundays, and his eye passed from one to another swiftly, but with a distinguishing regard of which he had never been conscious before, and their names swept across his memory like sudden flashes of light. There sat his own children, and his eye rested fondly upon them as they looked up to him; and he smiled tenderly to himself as his glance caught the flushed and fervent face of Jessica.

The sermon he had prepared during the week was one of great research, and of studied oratory, which should hold his hearers in strained and breathless attention; but as he bowed down his head in silent supplication for the blessing of God, he said to himself, "I will preach to this people from the saying of Christ, 'He calleth His own sheep by name, and leadeth them out.'"[1]

---

1 John 10:3.

CHAPTER II

IT'S ONLY A STROKE

he first part of the service passed by as usual, disturbed only by the occasional rustle of a silk dress, or the carefully hushed footstep up the aisles of some late comer; and the moment for the prayer before the sermon had come. Every head was bent, and a deep stillness prevailed, which grew more and more profound as the minister's voice still remained silent, as if he was waiting until there was no stir or rustle or movement to be heard throughout the congregation.

There was something awful in this solemn pause before his voice was lifted up to God; and as it prolonged itself, a sigh, it might have been from the minister's inmost heart, was heard by those nearest to the pulpit. One or two looked up, and saw his head bowed down, with the softened light of the lamps falling upon the silvery streaks of his hair, and they dropped their faces again upon their hands waiting. Then there ran a thrill and a shiver through all the congregation, and here and there a sob which could no longer be repressed broke the laboring silence.

After that there were whispers and murmurs, and faces lifted up with a vague dread upon them; and still the minister did not raise his face from the crimson cushion that his voice might allay the growing agitation. His children were looking up at last; and Jessica had risen from her knees, and was gazing up with eager eyes to his drooping head.

There was a stir now, and the spell of silence was broken; while Jessica, forgetful of everything but her deep love for him, ran swiftly up the steps and touched him timidly with her hand. The minister neither spoke nor moved.

The great congregation was in a tumult instantly, standing up, and talking, and crying out with hysterical sobs, and pushing out of their pews, and thronging towards the pulpit. In a few minutes the minister was carried down into the vestry, and the crowd gathered about the doors of it. Some of the chief men belonging to the chapel urged the congregation to disperse and return to their homes; but they were too much excited to leave before it was known what had befallen the minister.

Jessica pushed her way—being small and nimble, and used to crowds—to the very door of the vestry, where Daniel stood to guard it from being invaded by too many strangers; and she waited there beside him until the door was opened by a hand-breadth, and a physician whispered from within, "It is not death, but a stroke."

More quickly than the words could be carried from lip to lip among the crowd, Jessica glided through the midst to the pew where the minister's children were kneeling with their arms about one another, sobbing out inarticulate prayers to God. She stood for a moment beside them, scarcely knowing what to say, and then she fell down on her knees by Winny, and put her lips close to her ear.

"Miss Winny," she said with a trembling voice, "the

doctor says it's nothing but a stroke. He isn't taken with death, Miss Jane; it's only a stroke."

The children started up eagerly and caught Jessica's hands, clinging to her as some one older and wiser than themselves. They had had no bitter taste of life's troubles before this, for their mother had been taken from them before they were old enough to understand their loss, and their lives had been tenderly smoothed and cared for. That Jessica should bring them some intelligence and consolation in their sudden panic of dread invested her with a kind of superiority; so now they looked to her as one who could help and counsel them.

"What is a stroke, Jessica?" asked Jane, looking imploringly towards her with her white face.

"I don't hardly know," answered Jessica. "I know what strokes used to be when I lived with mother; but this is different, Miss Jane; this stroke comes from God, and it cannot be very bad."

The children were all three of them silent after Jessica had spoken; but each one of them was gathering comfort and strength from her words. It was a stroke which had come from God, and therefore it could not be very bad. No one had seen it fall; no one had known that the Father's hand was lifted up to strike, and it had come down softly and gently, only hushing the voice and shutting up the gateways of the senses. Now that it was known, the chapel was gradually emptying as the congregation went away, and Jane and Winny, feeling calmed and strengthened, were ready to listen to their nurse, who was now anxious to take them home.

"Let Jessica come home with us, nurse," said Winny, who still held Jessica's hand between both her own. The nurse consented willingly, and in a few minutes they were walking homewards, one on each side of Jessica. They felt strangely bewildered still; but Jessica was like a guide to them, leading them through the fog and over the slimy crossings with familiar confidence, until they reached the door of the minister's house, when she hung back shyly, as if not meaning to go in with them.

"You musn't leave us yet," cried Winny, impetuously. "Papa is not come home, and I'm a little bit afraid. Aren't you afraid, Jessica?"

"No," answered Jessica, cheerfully. "It can't be anything dreadful bad."

"You must come in and stay with us," said Jane, the calm sedateness of her manner a little shaken by her fears. "Nurse, we will take Jessica into papa's study till he comes home."

The three children went quietly up stairs to the study, and sat down by the fire, which was burning brightly, as if waiting to welcome the minister's return after the labors of the day. The minister had gathered about him many books, so that every part of the large room was filled with them.

On the table lay those which he had been studying during the week while he was preparing his elaborate sermon, which was to have astonished and electrified even his accustomed hearers; and upon the desk there were scattered about the slips of paper upon which he had jotted down some of the profound thoughts which only a few of his people could comprehend. But upon the chimney-piece, at the end where his easy-chair was placed, and close to his hand, lay a small pocket-Bible, so worn with much reading that there was no book in his study like it.

The troubled children sitting on the hearth knew nothing of the profound and scholarly volumes on the table; but they were familiar with the little Bible, and Winny, taking it in her hand, lifted it to her lips and kissed it fondly.

"Papa always used to read and talk to us on a Sunday night after we had come home," she said sorrowfully, speaking already as if the custom was one long past, which could never be resumed.

"Does a stroke last long, Jessica?" inquired Jane, with a look of deep anxiety.

"I'm not sure," answered Jessica. "Mother's strokes were sharp and soon over, but the smart lasted a long while. Maybe the stroke is now over, but perhaps the smart will last a little while. God knows."

"Yes," said Jane, the tears standing in her eyes, "and God knows what is best for papa and us. We've known that a long, long time, but now we must believe it with our hearts."

"Believing is a deal harder than knowing," remarked Winny, with a look wonderfully like her father's; and the three children were silent again, their minds full of thought, while they listened for the minister's return to his home.

CHAPTER III

JESSICA'S MOTHER

They were heavy steps which the three listening children heard at last in the hall below, and upon the staircase the sounds of carrying a helpless burden up the stairs, and Jane and Winny pressed closer to Jessica, who looked from one to the other with an air of tender encouragement. As the sounds drew nearer, they crept by one impulse to the door, and opening it a little way, they saw their father's face as he was carried past them, pale but peaceful, with the eyelids closed as if he were in a deep sleep. Jessica's quick eyes detected Daniel standing in the darkness at the end of the passage, and as soon as the sad procession had passed into the minister's chamber, and the door was shut, she darted out, and led him eagerly to the study.

"Oh, Standring!" cried Jane and Winny in one breath, "tell us everything about papa."

"Come, come, you needn't be frightened, my little ladies," answered Daniel, soothingly. "Please God, your papa will be all right again in a week or two. The doctors say he's been studying too much to make his grand sermons, and he hasn't given his brain rest enough. But he'll come all right again by-and-by, or I don't know whatever will become of the chapel."

"He won't die?" murmured Jane, with quivering lips.

"Die!—oh, no!" said Daniel. "Why, my dears, you're all of a tremble. It would be the best for you to go to bed, for you can't do any good sitting up."

"Standring," said Winny, "I wish you'd let Jessica stay all night with us. She could sleep with nurse; and our room is inside nurse's, and if we leave the door open we could talk to one another."

"She may stay and welcome, if nurse likes, Miss Winny," answered Daniel; and as the nurse was anxious for her children to feel their new sorrow as lightly as possible she was glad to grant their request.

So after a while it happened that Daniel was wending his way alone, through the fog and the damp of the streets, towards a little house in a quiet and respectable sort of court, where for the last three years he had dwelt with his adopted child. His mind had been fully occupied with the strange events of the night and the paralysis of his stricken master; but now that he was alone, and his thoughts were free to return to his own affairs, they suddenly recalled to him the minister's last words to himself.

What could it be of importance that he had to say to him when the evening service was finished? His brain had been busy with guesses, in spite of his conscience, during the singing of the hymns, and even during the first prayer, when he stood at the chapel-door to arrest the entrance of any late comer until it should be ended. Something of importance, and now the minister could not reveal it to him!

He knew that at a private committee meeting, during the past week, a plan had been proposed for erecting a small residence close to the new chapel and schoolrooms, where the chapel-keeper might dwell; and it had been suggested that his salary should be raised to such a sum as would free him from the necessity of seeking any other employment. In fact, the care of the chapel would be work enough, for it was to be very large and magnificent; and already his duties filled up four clear days of the week.

Could it be to speak about this the minister had desired him to come into his vestry immediately after the congregation had departed? But it was not so much the minister's business as that of the chief men belonging to the church. Could it be anything about Jessica? It did not seem very likely; yet the minister was very partial to Jessica, and always seemed pleased to see her about the vestry, and he was talking to her very kindly when Daniel went to fetch the pulpit books. It was a hard thing to pacify his awakened curiosity, and he supposed nobody could satisfy it but the minister himself. How long was the stroke likely to last?

Daniel was asking himself this question, which neither he nor any one else could answer, just as he reached the door of his dwelling. There was a dim light from a lamp at the entrance of the court, and there was the red gleam of his own fire shining upon the white window-blind within, so that he could distinguish pretty plainly the figure of a person, which looked more like a heap of rags, crouching upon his door-sill. A tattered coat was tied round the neck by the sleeves, and an old brimless hat was drawn over the back of the head; but the tangled hair, which hung in ragged locks over the face, was too long for a man's; and as he stooped down to look more closely, it was certainly a woman's face which was turned towards him.

"Come, come," he said, "you've no business here, you know; so you'd better get up and go home. You don't belong to this place, and you've made a mistake coming here. This is my house."

He had his key in his hand, ready to let himself in where the comfortable fire was waiting for him; but he could not open the door until the miserable creature had moved, and, though she raised herself a little, she did not get up on her feet.

"I don't belong to any place," she answered suddenly, yet fiercely; "and I haven't made any mistake in coming here. You're Daniel Standring, and I'm Jessica's mother."

Daniel reeled for an instant as if he had been struck by a very heavy blow. He had long ago ceased to trouble himself about Jessica's mother, or to dread her reappearance; and the minister had assured him that, if she should ever return to claim her daughter, he would use all his influence to protect Jessica from her, as being an unfit person to have the training of a child. The woman was standing up now, but leaning her back against his door, snapping her fingers at him with her face stretched out, with a glare of angry defiance in her bright eyes, which sparkled through the gloom.

"I've nearly had the door down," she said, with a hoarse laugh, "till all your neighbors came out to see what was the matter; but I scared them in again. The police himself turned tail like a coward." And she laughed again so loud that the quiet court seemed to ring with the sound, and a door or two was cautiously opened, and Daniel saw his neighbors peeping out, all of them decent people, who held him in high respect as the chapel-keeper of so fashionable a chapel.

"I want my daughter," she cried, in high, shrill notes, "my Jessica, my daughter. Where is she, you scoundrel?"

"Come, now, then," answered Daniel, emboldened by the advance of two or three of the men, who came up to form a flank of defense or resistance, "this behavior won't do. Jessica isn't here; so you'd better take yourself off. I wouldn't give her up to you if she was here; but she isn't here, and there's an end of it."

The woman seated herself once more upon the sill, and leaned her head against the door-post.

"If you go in, I go in," she said doggedly; "and if I stay out, you stay out, I want my Jessica."

It was an embarrassing position for Daniel. He did not like to resort to force in order to enter his house for several reasons. First, and chiefly, he was now too sincere a Christian to choose any violent or ungentle measures; but, besides this, the person before him was a woman, and the mother of Jessica; and he was himself in a softened mood, from the excitement and sorrow of the evening. He stretched out his arm, and fitted the key into the lock; but before he turned it he looked as closely as he could through the gloom into the woman's face.

"You're not drunk, are you?" he said.

"Neither sup nor drop has passed my lips today," she answered, with a groan of suffering.

"Well, well!—come in," said Daniel; "and you too, Mr.

Brookes, if you please. I'm not myself at all tonight; and it 'ud hearten me to have somebody to back me. Come in."

He opened the door into a comfortable and neat room, where everything was arranged with scrupulous order; for he was an orderly man by nature, and Jessica had already the thrifty habits of a housekeeper. The fire had been well raked over with small coals before he and Jessica started for chapel, and now it was a bank of glowing embers.

The woman tottered across to the hearth, and flung herself into Daniel's arm-chair. They could see now how wan and hollow her face was, with the cheeks fallen in, and the burning eyes sunk deep into the head, while, as she stretched out her thin and yellow hands over the fire, the red gleam shone through them. The poor tatters she wore were limp and dank with fog, and the slippers into which her naked feet were thrust were worn out at the toes, so as to give free inlet to the mud of the pavement.

Daniel regarded her in silence for a minute or two, and then he passed on into a small kitchen at the back, and returned quickly with some bread and cheese and some coffee, which he warmed up in a little saucepan. She drank the coffee eagerly, but she could not swallow more than a mouthful or two of the bread.

"And this is Jessica's home," she said, when she was revived a little; "and a very comfortable home too. Eh! but I'm a lucky mother, and she's a lucky girl. Will she be in tonight, Mr. Standring?"

"No," answered Daniel, shortly.

"Well, I can make myself comfortable," she said, with a laugh which made Daniel shiver. "I dare say her bed is softer than any I've slept on of late. Last night I slept under a scaffolding on some shavings. Don't put yourself out about me. I can make myself comfortable."

"But you cannot stay here all night," replied Daniel decisively.

"And why not?" she rejoined, "I suppose I'm as good as my daughter. Ah, she'll never be the woman I've been. I rode in my carriage once, man, I can tell you. And what should hinder me staying a night, or a week, or a month in your paltry little house? No, no! you'll not see my back tonight, I promise you."

"I wouldn't give you a night's lodging for five shillings," said Daniel, hastily.

"I'm not going to give you five farthings for it," said the woman, settling herself in his arm-chair with an air of impudent defiance. "Jessica's home is my home. If you turn me out, out she goes with me."

Daniel drew his neighbor aside into the kitchen, where he consulted with him in whispers, while he kept his eye upon his terrible visitor through the open door.

"What am I to do with her?" he asked. "I wouldn't have her stop here for anything. Jessica is staying all night with the minister's children; but she'll come back tomorrow. Whatever am I to do?"

"Give her some money to go away," answered Brookes; and after a little heavy-hearted hesitation Daniel resolved to act upon his advice. He returned into his comfortable little parlor, which in some way had never looked even to himself so comfortable and pleasant; and he addressed his visitor with a determined and resolute aspect.

JESSICA'S MOTHER IN DANIEL'S PARLOR.

"Now," he said, "if you won't go away peaceable I'll send for a policeman, as sure as I'm the chapel-keeper of St. John's Chapel. I don't want to be violent with you, for I'm a Christian man; but I don't know that a Christian man is bound to give you a lodging in his own house. I should rather think he wasn't. But if you will go away quiet, here is a shilling to pay for a bed and breakfast else-where. That's all I can do or say. It's that, or the police."

The woman deliberated for a few minutes, looking

hard into Daniel's face; but there was no sign of irresolution or relenting upon his grave features; and at last she raised herself slowly and weariedly from the chair, and dragged her slip-shod feet across the floor towards him. She took the shilling sullenly from his hand, and without a word passed out into the cold and damp of the streets, while Daniel watched her unsteady steps down the court with a feeling of relief.

But when Brookes was gone, and the door was locked for the night, and the agreeable warmth of the glowing fire wrapped round him, he could not keep his thoughts from wondering where the wretched woman had found a shelter. His mind also looked onwards with misgiving to the future which lay immediately before him and Jessica; and again he lamented on his own account that he could not go for counsel to Jessica's other friend, the minister who had been stricken into silence and unconsciousness, even concerning interests still nearer and dearer to his heart.

CHAPTER IV

JESSICA'S CHOICE

arly the next morning Daniel went to the minister's house, half hoping that he should hear that the malady of the night before had been only a temporary insensibility, from which he had recovered. But the minister lay in the same state of unconsciousness, and showed no sign of returning life. The nurse told him that a ragged and miserable woman, who called herself Jessica's mother, had seen him during the Sunday afternoon, and held a long conversation with him, after which he had ordered some food to be given her in the kitchen.

This, then, no doubt was the subject upon which the minister wished to speak to Daniel; and the latter felt more than ever lost in doubt as to what he ought to do, as it was now impossible to hear the advice which his master had intended to give to him.

He walked thoughtfully towards the chapel, with Jessica beside him, scarcely knowing how to break the news to her. She was a little sad and less talkative than usual, and her small hand was thrust lovingly into his own, as if she felt that it was needful to assure herself that it could return her warm grasp. When they opened the vestry-door, and, going in, saw all the confusion which bore testimony of the last night's calamity, Daniel drew the child closer to him with his arm, and bending down stiffly, kissed her uplifted face.

"He isn't going to die," said Jessica, with a trembling voice; "he is only resting himself, the doctor says, and then he will know us again, and speak to us all."

"To think!" cried Daniel, in a mournful amazement, "that he should have spoken thousands and thousands of words, ay! millions! and I scarce gave an ear to them; and now I'd almost offer a golden guinea for every word he could speak to me! Ay! Jessica, so that he spoke pretty short and simple, I'd give a guinea a word if he could tell me what I ought to do."

"Do you want him to say something particular?" asked Jessica.

"Ay! very particular," answered Daniel.

"Couldn't you ask God?" suggested Jessica.

"Well," he answered, doubtfully, "of course I could; but then there's no direct answer, which I couldn't mistake. My mother used to open her Bible, and take the first words she set eyes on for answer; and very queer answers they were sometimes. I'm not good enough yet to expect a very clear answer to my prayers."

Jessica made no answer, for Daniel's mode of reasoning was a little obscure to her; but she set to work to put the scattered chairs in order, while Daniel looked on with loving but troubled eyes.

"Jessica," he said, "the trouble I'd like to talk to him about is that your mother's come back again."

She started, and looked at him with great, wide-open eyes of amazement and terror, while her face quivered,

and she twitched her small shoulders a little, as if already
shrinking from a blow. But the expression of pain and
fear passed away quickly, and though her face was pale a
smile came upon it.

"Doesn't God know that mother's come back?" she
asked.

There was no need for Daniel to answer her question,
but he turned it over and over again in his own mind with
something very much like doubt. It seemed as if it would
have been so much better, especially at this crisis, for
Jessica's mother to remain absent; that it was as if God
had given up His particular providence over the affairs
of insignificant people like himself and Jessica. It would
be no wonder if amid all the affairs of the hosts of angels,
and the myriads of worlds of which he had a vague idea,
that God should overlook a little matter like the tramp-
ing to and fro of a drunken woman. It was a saddening
thought; but Daniel was in the mood to cherish it.

"Do you know where mother is?" asked Jessica.

"No, deary," answered Daniel. "I gave her a shilling
last night to pay for her lodging and breakfast. She told
me she'd had nothing to eat or drink all day; but the nurse
said she'd been to see the minister yesterday afternoon,
and had a good meal. She's sure to come again."

"Ay, she's sure to come again," echoed Jessica.

"And so," continued Daniel, "nurse and me have agreed
you'd better stay with the young ladies for a bit, out of the
way like, till I can see how I can settle with your mother.
You'd be glad to stay with Miss Jane and Winny, Jessica?"

"Yes," she answered, her face quivering again, as if

she could scarcely keep herself from crying; "but I'd like to see my mother."

"See your mother!" repeated Daniel, with unfeigned astonishment; "whatever for, Jessica?"

"She's my mother," replied Jessica, "and the Lord Jesus Christ had a mother. Oh! I'd like to see her again, and tell her about God, and Jesus Christ, and heaven. Perhaps she'd become a good woman!"

She could control herself no longer, and throwing herself on her knees before the minister's chair she hid her face in her hands, and Daniel heard that amid her sobs she was murmuring some prayer to God for her mother. This was a new perplexity, that Jessica should wish to see her cruel and hard-hearted mother; but there was something in it which he could neither blame nor gainsay.[1] He would rather have kept Jessica in safety at the minister's house than have her exposed to the frequent and violent visits of the drunken woman to his own little dwelling; but if Jessica decided otherwise he would not oppose her. His house did not seem the same place without her presence in it.

"Choose for yourself, deary," he said, very gently; "come home with me, and run the chance of your mother coming again soon; or go back to Miss Jane and Winny, who are so fond of you, and where everything is fine, and you'll be in such good company. Choose for yourself."

"I'll go home with you," said Jessica, getting up from her knees with a cheerful smile. "I couldn't think this morning who'd sweep the kitchen, and get the breakfast.

---

1 Gainsay—to contradict; to deny.

I'd rather go home with you, if you please."

It was impossible for Daniel not to be gratified at Jessica's choice, however troubled he might be with the idea of her mother's disturbance of their peace; for home was not home without her. They kept very near to one another all day at their work, and it was late at night before they returned home, where they found no one sitting upon the doorstep, as Daniel timorously[1] expected. But their neighbor Brookes informed them that Jessica's mother had been sobbing and crying before the closed door during a great part of the evening.

---

1 Timorous—fearful of danger; timid.

CHAPTER V

HOW A CHRISTIAN OUGHT TO ACT

Daniel was very anxious that Jessica should not be exposed to her mother's violence at any time during his absence, when he would not be there to protect her from any ill-usage; and as he was almost constantly engaged with the chapel affairs for the next two or three days, he and Jessica were never at home until late in the evening.

But upon Thursday night as they turned into the court Jessica's quick eye saw a woman's figure leaning against the door-post of their house. She stood still for an instant, clasping Daniel's hand with close and timid grasp and then, quitting him, she ran forward, and stretching out both her hands almost as if she wished to throw herself into her mother's arms, she cried, "Mother! mother!"

The woman laughed loudly and shrilly, and flung her shriveled arms about Jessica, fondling her with a maudlin fondness; Jessica drew back sorrowfully, and lifted herself on tip-toe to whisper into Daniel's ear:

"She's a little drunk, you know," she said, "but she isn't very bad yet. She isn't furious. What shall we do?"

It was precisely the question Daniel was asking of himself, for he could not bear the idea of taking a drunken women into his respectable and orderly house; and yet, could he turn our Jessica's mother before Jessica's eyes?

He paused for some minutes before unlocking the door, while the woman continued to talk in a foolish strain to her child, but at last he felt compelled to open it, and she was the first to push her way in. She took possession again of his arm-chair, and tossed her old, tattered hat into a corner of the room, while he looked on in helpless and deep dismay.

"Mother," said Jessica, speaking to her in gentle but steady tones, "this isn't your house at all, and you can't stay here. It's Mr. Dan'el's house: but I dare say he'll let me give you some supper, and then you'd better go away, and come to see me again when you're quite yourself."

The woman fastened her red and sunken eyes upon Jessica, and then burst into a fit of passionate lamenting, while she drew the child closer to her.

"Oh! I wish I was a better woman!" she cried. "I've been driven to it, Jessica. But I'm coming to live here with you now, and be decent like the rest of you. I'm going to turn over a new leaf; and you'll see how steady I'll be. I'll be no disgrace to any of ye."

"But, mother," said Jessica, "you can't live here, because it's Mr. Dan'el's house, and he only took me out of charity, when I was ill and you left me. We can't look for him to take you."

"If you stay, I stay," said her mother, in a tone of obstinacy, setting her elbows firmly upon the arms of the chair, and planting her feet on the floor; "or, if I go, you go. I'd like to know who'd have the heart to separate a mother from her own child!"

Jessica stood for a minute or two looking at her

mother with eyes full of sadness and pity, and then she crept to Daniel's side, and whispered to him with an air of pleading.

"I don't think she ever knew that God is our Father," she said.

Daniel found himself at a complete loss as to what he ought to do. The miserable creature before him shocked every sense of decency and propriety, which had been firmly and rigidly rooted in his nature; and the very sight of her, drunken and disorderly, upon his hearth, was an abomination to him. Since she had last spoken, she had fallen into a brief slumber, and her grey, uncovered head was shaking and nodding with an imbecile aspect. Jessica was gone upstairs, for what he did not know, unless it was to make some arrangement for her mother's accommodation; and he remained motionless, staring at the wretched woman with a feeling of abhorrence and disgust which increased every moment.

But presently he heard Jessica's light step descending the stairs, and started with surprise when she came into the room. She had changed her tidy dress for the poorest and oldest clothing in her possession, and she approached him with a sorrowful but patient look upon her face.

"Mr. Dan'el," she said, unconsciously falling back into speaking the old name by which she had first called him, "you musn't go to take mother in out of charity, as well as me. That 'ud never do. So I'll go away with her tonight, and in the morning, when she's sober, I'll tell her all about God, and Jesus Christ, and heaven. She doesn't know it yet, but maybe when she hears everything she'll be a

different woman; like me, you know; and then we can all
help her to be good. Only I must go away with her tonight,
or she'll get into a raging fury like she used to do."

"No, no, no!" cried Daniel vehemently. "I couldn't let
you go, dear. Why, Jessica, I love you more than my money,
don't I? God knows I love you better. I'd rather lose all my
money, ay, and my place as chapel-keeper, than lose you,"

"You aren't going to lose me," said Jessica, with the
same patient but sorrowful light in her eyes, "I'm only
going away for a little while with my mother. She's my
mother, and I want to tell her all I know—that she may go
to heaven as well as us. I'll come back tomorrow."

"She shall stay here," said Daniel, hesitatingly.

"No, no," answered Jessica, "that 'ud never do. She'll be
for stopping always if you give in once. You'd better let me
go with her this one night; and tomorrow morning, when
she's all right, I'll tell her everything. She'll be very low
then, and she'll hearken to me. Mother! I'm ready to go
with you."

The woman opened her swollen eyelids and staggered
to her feet, laying her hand heavily upon the slight shoul-
der of Jessica, who looked from her to Daniel with a clear,
sad, brave smile, as she bent her childish shoulders a little under her mother's hand, as if they felt already the
heavy burden that was falling upon her life. It was a hard
moment for Daniel, and he was yet doubtful whether he
should let them both go, or keep them both; but Jessica
had led her mother to the door, and already her hand was
upon the latch.

"Stop a minute, Jessica," he said, "I'll let you go with

JESSICA TRYING TO MANAGE HER MOTHER.

her this once; only there's a lodging-house not far off, and I'll come with you, and see you safe for the night, and pay your lodgings."

"All right!" answered Jessica, with a quick, sagacious nod; and in a few minutes they were walking along the streets, Jessica between her mother and Daniel, all of them very silent, except when the woman broke out into a stave[1] or two of some old, long-forgotten song. Before

1 Stave—a metrical portion; a stanza.

long they reached the lodging-house of which Daniel had spoken, and he saw them safely into the little, close, dark closet, which was to be their bedroom.

"Good-night," said Daniel, kissing Jessica with more than usual tenderness; "you don't feel as if you'd like to come back with me, now we've seen your mother comfortable, do you?"

"No," answered Jessica, with a wistful look from him to her mother, who had thrown herself upon the bed and was fast asleep already, "I think I'm doing what God would like me to do; aren't I? He knows she is my mother."

"Ay, God bless you, my dear," said Daniel, turning away quickly, and closing the door behind him. He stumbled down the dark stairs into the street, and returned to his desolate home, saying to himself, "I'm sure I don't know how a Christian ought to act in this case; and there's nobody to go and ask now."

CHAPTER VI

DANIEL'S PRAYER

he two following days, Friday and Saturday, were always a busy time at the chapel, for the whole place had to be swept and dusted in preparation for the coming Sunday. Never had Daniel felt so depressed and down-hearted as when he entered the chilly and empty chapel early in the morning and alone, for Jessica was to follow him by-and-by, when her mother had strolled away for the day to her old haunts.

Only a week ago he and Jessica had gone cheerfully about their work together, Jessica's blithe,[1] clear young voice echoing through the place as she sang to herself, or called to him from some far-off pew, or down from the gallery. But now everything was upset, and in confusion. He mounted the pulpit steps, and after shaking the cushions, and dusting every ledge and crevice, he stood upright in a strange and solemn reverie, as he looked round upon the empty pews, which were want to be so crowded on a Sunday.

It would make a wonderful difference to the place, he thought, if anything worse should happen to his master; for even to himself Daniel could not bear to say the sad word, death. They could never find his like again. Never! he repeated, laying his hand reverently upon the crimson cushion, where the minister's grey head had sunk in

---

1 Blithe—merry or joyous.

sudden dumbness before God; and two large solemn tears forced themselves into Daniel's eyes, and rolled slowly down his cheeks.

He did not know who ever would fill the pulpit even on the coming Sabbath; but he felt that he could never bear to stay at the chapel after its glory was departed, and see the congregation dwindling down, and growing more and more scanty every week, until only a few drowsy hearers came to listen sleepily to a lifeless preacher. No! no! that would go a good way towards breaking his heart.

Besides all this, how he longed to be able to ask the minister what he ought to do about Jessica's mother! But whether for instruction in the pulpit or for counsel in private the minister's voice was hushed; and Daniel's heart was not a whit lighter, as he slowly descended the pulpit steps.

It was getting on for noon before Jessica followed him, bringing his dinner with her in a little basket. Her eyes were red with tears, and she was very quiet while he ate with a poor appetite the food she set before him. He felt reluctant to ask after her mother; but when the meal was finished Jessica drew near to him, and took hold of his hand in both her own.

"Mr. Daniel," she said, very sorrowfully, "when mother awoke this morning I told her everything about Jesus Christ, and God, and heaven; and she knew it all before! Before I was born, she said!"

"Ah!" ejaculated Daniel, but not in a tone of surprise; only because Jessica paused and looked mournfully into his face.

"Yes," continued Jessica, shaking her head hopelessly, "she knew about it, and she never told me, never! She never spoke of God at all, only when she was cursing. I don't know now anything that'll make her a good woman. I thought that if she only heard what I said she'd love God, but she only laughed at me, and said it's an old story. I don't know what can be done for her now."

Jessica's tears were falling fast again, and Daniel did not know how to comfort her. There was little hope, he knew, of a woman so enslaved by drunkenness being brought back again to religion and God.

"If the minister could only see her!" said Jessica. "He speaks as if he had seen God, and talked to him sometimes; and she'd be sure to believe him. I don't know how to say the right things."

"No, no!" answered Daniel. "She saw him on Sunday, before he had the stroke, and he talked a long time to her. No! she won't be changed by him."

"She's my mother, you know," repeated Jessica anxiously.

"Ay!" said Daniel, "and that puzzles me, Jessica; I don't know what to do."

"Couldn't we pray to God," suggested Jessica, again, "now, before we go on any farther?"

"Maybe it would be the best thing to do," agreed Daniel, rising from his chair and kneeling down with Jessica beside him. At first he attempted to pray like some of the church-members at the weekly prayer meeting, in set and formal phrases; but he felt that if he wished to obtain any real blessing he must ask for it in simple and childlike words, as if speaking face to face with his Heavenly Father; and this was the prayer he made, after freeing himself from the ceremonial etiquette of the prayer meetings:

"Lord, thou knowest that Jessica's mother is come back, and what a drunken and disorderly woman she is, and we don't know what to do with her, and the minister cannot give us his advice. Sometimes I'm afraid I love my money too much yet, but, Lord, if it's that, or anything else that's hard in my heart, so as to hinder me from doing what the Savior, Jesus Christ, would do if he was in my place, I pray thee to take it away, and make me see clearly what my Christian duty is. Dear Lord, I beseech thee keep both me and Jessica from evil."

Daniel rose from his knees a good deal relieved and lightened in spirit. He had simply, with the heart of a child, laid his petition before God; and now he felt that it was God's part to direct him. Jessica herself seemed brighter, for if the matter had been laid in God's hands she felt that it was certain to come out all right in the end.

They went back to their work in the chapel, and though it was melancholy to remember that their own minister would be absent from the pulpit on the Sunday which was drawing near, they felt satisfied with the thought that God knew all, and was making all things work together for the good of those who loved him.

CHAPTER VII

A BUSY DAY FOR DANIEL

Daniel went home with Jessica, still disturbed a little with the dread of finding his unwelcome visitor awaiting their arrival; but she was not there, and there was no interruption to their quiet evening together, though both of them started and looked towards the door at every sound of a footstep in the court.

After they had their tea, and while Jessica was putting away the tea-things in the kitchen, Daniel unlocked his desk, and took out his receipts for the money he had out on interest. Since he had adopted Jessica he had not added much to his savings; for besides the cost of her maintenance there had also been the expenses of housekeeping. In former times he had scarcely cared how uncomfortable his lodgings were, provided that they were cheap; and he had found that to have a tidy and comfortable house of his own involved a great outlay of money.

Sometimes a thought had crossed his mind, of which he was secretly ashamed, that the minister, who seemed so fond of Jessica, or at least some of the rich members of the congregation, might have borne part of the charge of her living; but no one had ever offered to do anything for her. He had spent his money with a half grudge, and now the question upon his mind was, did God require him to waste—he said "waste" to himself—his hardly-earned savings upon a drunken and wicked woman?

It was a hard trial. He loved Jessica, as he had said, more than his money, and he had never really regretted taking her into his home; she was like a daughter to him, and he was a happier and a better man for her companionship. But this woman was an abhorrence to him, a disgust and disgrace. She had no more claim upon him than any other of the thousands of lost men and women who thronged the streets of London.

Surely God did not require him to take this money, which was the sole provision for his old age; and now that the minister was so stricken there would be no new chapel built for him, and no house for the chapel-keeper, and no increase of salary. That was already a settled point, for the physicians who were attending the minister declared positively that never again would his over-worked brain be capable of sustaining any long strain of thought, such as had drawn together his eager and attentive congregations.

It was scarcely even a question whether he would be able to resume his position as pastor of this old church; and under a new minister it was probable the place might be half emptied, and his emoluments[1] as chapel-keeper be considerably lessened. He was getting older too, and there was not more than ten years' work in him. He looked at his treasured receipts, and asked himself, Could it be possible that God required him to sacrifice his past gains, and risk his future comforts upon Jessica's mother?

Then another question, in the very depths of his conscience, was whispered to his heart, which at first was

---

1 Emolument—the profit arising from office or employment.

willing to remain deaf to the small and quiet voice; but it grew louder and more clamorous, until Daniel found that it must be heard and answered.

"What think you Christ would have done with this woman?" it asked. If God had brought her to that door where He dwelt as a poor carpenter, would he have thrust her back upon the misery of the life which drove her again and again to the vilest of her sins? Would Jesus, who came to seek as well as to save those who are lost, have balanced a book of savings against the hope, faint though it was, of rescuing the woman's soul?

"Daniel, Daniel," answered the quiet voice to his inmost heart, "what would thy Lord have done?" He tried to set it aside, and hush it up, while he turned the key upon his receipts, telling himself that he had done all that his duty as a Christian demanded of him when he rescued and adopted Jessica. But the Spirit of God has a gracious tyranny which requires more and more from the soul which begins to sacrifice itself. He had mastered his love of money for the sake of a child whom he loved; now he must conquer it to rescue a wretched woman whom he shrank from.

The struggle seemed to last long, but it was ended before Jessica came back to the fireside. Daniel's prayer in the afternoon had been too sincere for him to be left in darkness to grope along a wrong path. His face wore a smile as Jessica took her sewing and sat down opposite to him; such a smile as rarely lit up his rigid features.

"Jessica," he said, "God has shown me what to do."

"Perhaps it'll be better than the minister himself," answered Jessica.

"Ay!" answered Daniel. "I don't think the minister could have told me plainer. Why, Jessica, suppose the Lord had been living here, and your mother had come to his door, wouldn't he have cared for her, and grieved over her, and done everything he could to prevent her going on in sin? Well, dear, it seems to me it wouldn't be altogether right to take her to live with us all at once, because you are a young girl and ought not to see such ways, and I might get angry with her; but I'll hire a room for her somewhere, that shall be always kept for her, and whenever she comes to it there will be a bed, and a meal for her; and we'll be very kind to her, and see if by any means we can help to make her good."

Jessica had dropped her sewing and drawn near to Daniel; and now she flung her arms round his neck, and hid her face upon his breast, crying.

"Why, now, now, my dear!" said Daniel, "what ails you, Jessica? Wouldn't the Lord Jesus have made a plan something like that? Come, come, we'll pray to him to make her a good woman; and then—who knows?—she may come here to live with us."

"She's my own mother, you know," sobbed Jessica, as if those words alone were thoughts in her heart.

"Yes!" answered Daniel, "and we must do our best for her. Jessica, I know now that I love God more than aught else in this world or the next."

It was a knowledge worth more than all the riches of earth; and as Daniel sat in his chimney-corner he could hardly realize his own happiness. To be sure that he loved God supremely, and to have the witness in himself that he did so! He felt as if he could take all the world of lost and ruined sinners to his heart, and, like Christ himself, lay down his life for them. There was only one shadow, if it could be called a shadow, upon his joy unspeakable, and full of comfort—it was that he could not gladden the heart of the minister by telling him of this change in his nature.

The next day was a very busy one for Daniel; for besides his ordinary duties he charged himself with finding a suitable place for Jessica's mother. He met with a room at last in the dwelling of a poor widow, who was glad to let him have it on condition that he paid the rent of the house.

He and Jessica bought a bed and a chair and a table, and put everything in readiness for their expected visitor. Scanty as was the furniture, it was a warm and certain shelter for the poor vagrant, who spent half her night shivering under archways, or in unfinished buildings; and never had Daniel felt so pure a gratification as when he gave a last look at the room, and taking Jessica by the hand went back to his own home, no longer afraid of meeting the woman on his threshold.

CHAPTER VIII

HOPES OF RECOVERY

I t was a happy Sunday for Daniel, in spite of the minister's absence and the downcast looks of the congregation as they occupied their accustomed seats. The chapters read out of the Bible had new meaning for him, and the singing brought happy tears to his eyes. It seemed as if he had never truly known God before; and though the sermon, by a student merely, was one which he would have criticized with contempt a week ago, now it was pleasant only to hear the names of his God and Savior; just as one is pleased to hear even a stammering tongue speak the praises of those we love.

During the evening service Jessica went to stay with the minister's children. Jane came down to her in the hall and told her they were to sit in their father's room while the strange nurse and their own nurse were having tea together in an adjoining room.

"Nurse thinks," said Jane, "that, if papa knew, he would like us to sit with him this Sunday evening; and sometimes we think he does know, though he never speaks, and he seems to be asleep all the time. We are to read our chapter and say our hymns just as if he could hear. And nurse says he told your mother only last Sunday that he loves you almost like one of his own little girls. So we said we should like you to come and read with us; for you are not a bit afraid, Jessica."

They had mounted the stairs while Jane was whispering these sentences; and now, hand in hand, they entered the minister's room.

There was a fire burning, and a lamp lit upon a table, so that the minister's face could be plainly seen, as they stole with tender caution to his side.

It had been a pale face always, but it was very colorless now; the lids were closed lightly over the eyeballs, which seemed almost to burn and shine through them; and the lips, which might have been speaking words that seemed to bring his listeners almost into the presence of God, were locked in silence. Yet the face was full of life, which rippled underneath as it were, as if the colorless cheeks, and thin eyelids, and furrowed forehead were only a light mask; and while the children gazed upon it the lips moved slowly, but soundlessly.

"He is talking to God," whispered Jessica, in a tone of awe.

"Jessica," said Winny, pressing close to her, "I can't help thinking about Paul, when he was caught up into the third heaven and heard unspeakable words. I think perhaps he looked like my father."

She had never called him father before, and she uttered it in a strangely solemn voice, as if it was a more fitting title than the familiar one they had called him by on ordinary days. They stood beside him for a few minutes, and then they crept on tiptoe across to the hearth. The children read their chapter, and said their hymns, and sang a favorite one of their father's, in soft, low tones which could scarcely have been heard outside the room; and the little timepiece over the fireplace chimed seven as they finished.

"It was just this time last Sunday," said Jane, "when papa had the stroke. He was just going to pray when the chapel-clock struck seven."

"I wonder what he was going to say?" said Winny, sorrowfully.

"Our Father!" murmured a voice behind them, very low and weak, like the voice of one who has only strength to utter a single cry; and turning quickly, with a feeling of fear, they saw their father's eyes opened, and looking towards them with inexpressible tenderness. Jessica laid her finger on her lips, as a sign to them to be still, and with timid courage she went to the minister's side.

"Do you know us again?" she asked, trembling between fear and joy: "do you know who we are, minister?"

"Jessica, and my children," he whispered, with a feeble smile fluttering upon his face.

"He is come back!" cried Jessica, returning with swift but noiseless steps to Jane and Winny. "Let us make haste and tell the others. Maybe he is hungry and weak and faint. But he knows us—he is come back to us again."

In a few minutes the joyful news was known throughout the house, and was carried to the chapel before the evening service was over; and the congregation, as they dispersed, spoke of their minister's recovery hopefully. It was the crowning gladness of the day to Daniel, and he lingered at the minister's house, to which he hastened as soon as he had closed the chapel, until it was getting on

FIRST SIGN OF THE MINISTER'S RECOVERY.

for midnight; and then he left Jessica with the children, and started off for his home, with a heart in which joy was full.

CHAPTER IX

THE GATE OF DEATH

Daniel had a good way to go, for the minister's house was in an opposite direction to his own from the chapel. The November fogs still hung about London, and the lamps gave only a dim light through the gloom. Those who were yet walking about the streets marched quickly, as if anxious to reach whatever shelter they called their own.

Daniel himself was making his way as fast as he could along the muddy pavement, when he came to a part of the streets where the drainage was being repaired, and where charcoal fires were burning in braziers here and there, at once to give warning to the passers-by and to afford warmth to the watchmen who stayed beside them all night. One of the watchmen had brought an old door, and reared it up against a rude wall of stone and bricks, so as to form some protection from the rain, which now and then fell in short showers.

He had quitted his shed for some reason or other, and as Daniel drew near his steps were arrested; for crouching underneath it, and stretching out her shriveled arms over the brazier full of charcoal, was Jessica's mother. The fitful light was shining strongly upon her face, and showed the deep lines which misery and degradation had ploughed upon it and the sullenness and stupidity which

MIDNIGHT.

were stamped upon her features.

He stood still, gazing at her with disgust; but very soon a feeling of profound pity took its place. He had been wondering what had become of her since Friday morning, and had even felt a kind of anxiety about her; and now, as he thought of the room with its comfortable bed which was waiting for her, instead of the brief shelter of the shed, he climbed over the heaps of rubbish which lay between them, calling to her, for he did not know her name, "Jessica's mother!"

The woman started to her feet at the sound of his voice, and looked him full in the face with an expression of utter wretchedness. Her eyes were inflamed and swollen with tears, and every feature was quivering as if she had no control over them. She was so miserable a creature that Daniel did not know in what words to speak to her; but his heart was moved with an unutterable compassion, unknown to him till now.

He even felt a sympathy for her, as if he had once been in the same depths of degradation, as he looked down shudderingly into the deep abyss where she had fallen by her sins; and the sense of her misery touched him so closely that he would have given his life for her salvation. He stretched out his hand towards her, but she pushed it away, and with a groan of despair she fled from the light, and sought to hide herself in the darkness of the foggy streets.

But Daniel was not easily turned aside from his desire to bring some help to Jessica's mother, even if it were no more than to rescue her from the chilliness of the November night. He followed her with steps as rapid as her own, and only that she had had the first start he would have been quickly at her side. She fled swiftly along the streets to escape from him, and he pursued her, hoping that she would soon weary, and would turn to speak to him.

But she kept on until Daniel found himself at the entrance of one of the old bridges of the city which span the wide waters of the river. Side by side with it a new

bridge was being constructed, with massive beams of tim-
ber, and huge blocks of stone, and vast girders of iron,
lying like some giant skeleton enveloped in the fog, yet
showing dimly through it by the glare of red lights and
blazing torches, which were kindled here and there, and
cast flickering gleams upon the black waters beneath, into
which Daniel looked down with a shiver, as he paused for
a moment in his pursuit.

But he had lost sight of the woman when he lifted up
his eyes again, unless the strange dark figure on one of
the great beams stretching over the river was the form
of Jessica's mother. He pressed towards it, quitting the
safety of the old bridge; but, as a wild and very mournful cry smote upon his ear, he missed his footing, and fell
heavily upon a pile of masonry at some distance below
him.

It could only have been a minute that he was uncon-
scious, for the deep-toned clock of St. Paul's had chimed
the first stroke of midnight as he lost footing, and the
boom of the last stroke was still ringing through the air
when he tried to raise himself and look again for the dark
figure which he had seen hanging over the river; but he
could not move, and he lay quietly, without making a second effort, and thinking clearly over what had happened.

There was little doubt that the wretched woman, whom
he had sought to save, had hurried away from all salvation, whether of God or man; and yet how was it that,
instead of the shock of horror, a perfect peace possessed
his soul? For a moment it seemed to him that he could
hear a voice speaking, through the dull and monotonous

splashing of the cold water against the arches below him, and it said to him, "Because thou hast been faithful unto death, I will give thee a crown of life."[1]

Was he going to die? he asked himself, as a pang of extreme agony ran through all his frame, and extorted a moan from his lips. He was ready and willing, if it was the will of God; but he would like to see his little Jessica again and tell her gently with his own lips that her mother was dead, and gone—he could say nothing gentler—to her own place, which God knew of.

The midnight hour was quieter than usual in the busy city, for it was Sunday and the night was damp; so Daniel lay for some time before he heard the tread of a passer-by upon the bridge above him. He could hear many sounds at a little distance; but he could not raise his voice loudly enough to be audible through the splash of the waters. But as soon as he heard footsteps upon the bridge he cried, with a strong effort, "Help me, or I shall die before morning!"

It seemed a long time, and one of great suffering to him, before he was raised up and laid upon the smooth pathway of the bridge. But he did not cry out or groan; and as the little crowd which gathered around him spoke in tones of commiseration[2] and kindness, he thanked them calmly, and with a cheerfulness which deceived them. They bore him to the nearest hospital, but as they would have laid him on a bed there he stopped them, with great energy and earnestness.

---

1 Revelation 2:10.
2 Commiseration—pity; compassion.

"Let the doctor see me first," he said, "and tell me whether I am likely to die or live."

The doctor's hand touched him, and there were a few questions put to him, which he answered calmly; and then, as the doctor looked down upon him with a grave face, he looked back with perfect composure.

"I'm a Christian man," said Daniel, "and I'm not afraid to die. But if you think there's no chance for me I'd rather go home. I've a little girl at home who'd like to be with me all the time till I'm taken away from her. The key of my house is in my pocket. Let me be taken home."

They could not refuse his request; but the doctor told him he might live yet for some days, though the injuries he had received gave no hope of his life; to which Daniel replied only by a solemn smile. It was nearly morning before he reached his house, under the care of a nurse and a student from the hospital; and thus he entered for the last time the home where he had spent the three happiest years of his life with Jessica.

CHAPTER X

SPEAK OF HIS LOVE

or several days Daniel suffered great pain, but with such perfect peace and joy in his heart that it seemed as if he could scarcely realize or feel his bodily anguish. Jessica was with him constantly; and when he was free from pain she read aloud to him, or talked with him of the heaven to which he was going, and which seemed to lie open to his gaze already, as one catches a glimpse from afar off some beautiful country basking in the glory of a full noontide sunshine.

The chapel people came to see him, some of them in the carriages which of old used to set him pondering upon their riches; and they left him, marveling that they had known so little of the religiousness of the man who had ushered them to their pews Sunday after Sunday. But as yet the minister had not visited him, though he had sent him word that as soon as it was possible he would come to see him.

The last day had arrived; both Daniel and Jessica knew that it was the last day, and she had not stirred from his side since morning; and still the minister had not come—had not been able to come to the death-bed of his old friend. For they were old friends, having met many times a week for a dozen years in the same chapel; and since Jessica had drawn them closer together the

learned and eloquent preacher had cared for Daniel's illit-
erate soul; and the chapel-keeper had learned to pick up
some crumbs of nourishment from the great feast which
the minister prepared week after week for his intellectual
congregation. He had not been, but Daniel was undis-
turbed, and so, patient and peaceful, with a smile upon
his lips when he met Jessica's wistful eyes, he waited for
the last hour and the last moment to come.

Yet before it was too late, and before his eye grew dim,
and his tongue numbed with the chillness of death, the
minister arrived, pale in face, and bowed down with weak-
ness, and with a trembling voice which faltered often as
he spoke. They clasped one another's hands, and looked
into one another's face with a strange recognition, as if
both had seen further into the other world than they had
ever done before, and then the minister sank feebly into
the chair beside Daniel's pillow.

"I will rest here, and stay with you for an hour," he
said.

"It is the last hour," answered Daniel.

"Be it so," replied the minister. "I too have looked
death in the face."

They were silent for a while, while the minister rallied
his strength, and then he bent his head, his head only, for
he was too feeble yet to kneel beside the dying man, and
he poured forth a prayer to God in his inmost heart, but
with hesitating lips, which no longer uttered with ready
speech the thoughts which thronged to his brain. The
Amen with which he ended was almost a groan.

"My power is taken from me," he said; "the Almighty

has stricken me in the pride of my heart. I shall never more speak as I used to do, of his glory and majesty, and the greatness of his salvation."

"You can speak of his love," murmured Daniel.

"Yes," he answered, despondently, "but only as a child speaks. I shall never stir the hearts of the congregation again. My speech will be contemptible."

"Jessica, tell him what you and I have been talking about," said Daniel.

Jessica lifted up her face from the pillow, and turned it towards the minister, a smile struggling through her tears; and though her voice was unsteady to begin it grew calm and clear before she had spoken many words.

"We were talking how he'd never be the chapel-keeper any more, and go up into the pulpit to carry the books before you; and then we thought it was true, maybe, what the doctor says, that you'd never be well enough again to preach in such a big chapel; and so we went on talking about the time when we shall all be in heaven. We said perhaps God would give you more beautiful thoughts there, and grander words, and you'd still be our minister; and the angels 'ud all come thronging up in crowds all about you and us to hearken to what you'd thought about Jesus Christ and about God; and there'd be a great congregation again. Only whenever you were silent for a minute we could look up and see the Savior himself listening to us all."

Then the minister bowed his pale face upon his hands; but he did not answer a word.

"There's one thing still I want to say," said Daniel.

"I've made my will, and left all I had to Jessica; but I don't know where she'll find a home. If you'd look out for her—"

"Jessica shall come home to me," interrupted the minister, laying his hand upon hers and Daniel's and clasping them both warmly.

"I'm a Christian man," whispered Daniel. "I know that I love God, and that he has made me something like himself. There's a verse about it in the Bible."

"Beloved," said the minister, "'now are we the sons of God, and it doth not yet appear what we shall be; but we know that, when he shall appear, we shall be like him; for we shall see him as he is.'"[1]

There was no stammering of the minister's speech as he pronounced these words, and his face grew bright, as did the face of the dying man. Daniel's mind wandered a little, and he groped about, as in the dark, for the Bible, which lay upon the bed; and he murmured,

"It's time to take up the books, for the congregation is waiting, and the minister is ready. I will take them up to heaven."

He spoke no more; but the Bible after a while fell from his hand; and Jessica and the minister, looking upon his face, saw that in heaven he was beholding the face of the Father.

It proved true that the minister could never again preach a sermon such as in former times, when the people listened with strained attention, and he was to them as a very lovely song of one that hath a pleasant voice, and playeth well on an instrument; but they heard his words

---

1 1 John 3:2.

and did them not.[1] Yet he was a man of calmer happiness than before; and in his quiet country home, where sometimes of a Sunday he mounted the pulpit-steps of a little chapel, and taught a simple congregation simple truths, he drew nearer day by day in spirit to the great congregation who were waiting for him, and before whom his lips should never more be silenced.

1 Ezekiel 33:32

9329392R00038

Printed in Great Britain
by Amazon.co.uk, Ltd.,
Marston Gate.